EVERY SATURDAY

Written and Illustrated
by Alyse Newman

PRICE STERN SLOAN, INC.

To Walter, Jim and Lucky

Library of Congress Cataloging-in-Publication Data

Newman, Alyse.
  Every Saturday.

  Summary: The quarrelsome residents of a neighborhood postpone their
bickering when a parrot steals Mr. Small's silverware.

  [1. Neighborhood—Fiction]   I. Title.
PZ7.N4796Ev 1987   [E]   87-3615
  ISBN 0-8431-1944-6

Copyright © 1987 by Alyse Newman
Published by Price Stern Sloan, Inc.
360 North La Cienega Boulevard, Los Angeles, California 90048

Every Saturday Mr. Bellini, a warmhearted, bird-loving man, would walk to the park to feed the pigeons. And every Saturday he would leave his dog at home because his dog would chase the pigeons away. "See you in a little while," Mr. Bellini would say as he went out. And every Saturday Mr. Bellini would forget to leave food for his dog, whose name was Caruso, by the way.

Caruso knew Mr. Bellini would not be gone for long. But Caruso did like to have a little snack. So every Saturday Caruso would go over to the Gooches' yard and eat their cat's food. Then Caruso would go home and sleep until Mr. Bellini's return.

Every Saturday the Gooches' cat, whose name was Mabel, by the way, would discover that her food had been eaten. So Mabel would go next door to the Smalls' yard and rummage through the Smalls' garbage which she always knocked over.

Every Saturday the Small family, whose names were Mom, Pop, Elvira, Napoleon and Porkchop, would accuse the Gooches of having a can-dumping, garbage-picking cat.

The Gooches, whose names were Gilbert and Rona, by the way, would never believe that Mabel was a garbage picker. The Gooches would call the Smalls big liars and say it was the Smalls' fault that the neighborhood looked and smelled utterly awful.

Every Saturday the other
neighbors would come out and take
sides. Then everyone would start to argue
and someone would call for the police.
Every Saturday the policeman, whose name was
Officer Dowdy, by the way, would arrive on his horse.
Officer Dowdy would tell everyone to simmer down.
And after awhile they would...until the next Saturday.

One Saturday the Smalls were having an extra-special Saturday brunch of seven pizza pies. Like every Saturday the Gooches' cat knocked over the garbage cans. The Smalls were such loud chewers they couldn't hear the racket outside. Porkchop, the dog, heard it, but she only barked once and stayed by the table to beg for food.

When the garbage started to smell, the Smalls knew that Mabel, the cat, had struck again. Like every Saturday the Smalls, including Porkchop, the dog, went to the Gooches to complain about Mabel.

Like every Saturday the Smalls and the Gooches exchanged unkind words. The other neighbors came out and took sides. Then everyone started to quarrel and someone had to call for the police. Officer Dowdy arrived on his horse, whose name was Lily, by the way.

But *this* Saturday, while Officer Dowdy was telling everyone to simmer down, a robber was in the Smalls' house. And this was very *un*like every Saturday.

The robber, who was actually a rather rare bird, was stealing as much of the Smalls' silverware as could fit into his knapsack. The knapsack, by the way, happened to have an un-mended hole.

Elvira Small saw him taking off and shouted, "THIEF!" But Elvira Small had a very small voice and with all the shouting people outside nobody could possibly hear her. So it seemed the thief, whose name was Angus Macaw, by the way, would get away scot-free.

Then Porkchop, the dog, heard Elvira and alerted the other Smalls who hollered, "HELP! POLICE! THIEF!"

Although he was very nearby, Officer Dowdy couldn't help the Smalls. He couldn't even hear them. He was still attempting to settle the neighborhood squabble which had grown very, very noisy.

The Smalls tried pursuing the thief themselves but after their extra-special Saturday brunch they couldn't run. So it was Porkchop, the dog, who chased after the thief.

Angus Macaw, the thief, had not gone far. The silverware was weighing him down and he couldn't fly. The best he could do was to run, using his wings to propel him along. Soon Porkchop, the dog, was close on his trail.

She hounded Angus Macaw, the thief, through gardens, over fences, under shrubbery, on top of parked cars,

into sprinklers, up and down see-saws, around baby strollers,
in front of lawn mowers

and all the way into the park...the very park where
Mr. Bellini was sitting.

Like every Saturday, Mr. Bellini was settled on his favorite
bench, tossing food to the pigeons. Suddenly Angus Macaw, the
thief, jumped onto the bench. He smashed Mr. Bellini's pigeon food,
squashed Mr. Bellini's left hand and squished Mr. Bellini's hat as he dashed by.

As soon as Angus Macaw, the thief, jumped off the bench, Porkchop, the dog, jumped on! She crashed over Mr. Bellini's smashed pigeon food, squashed left hand and squished hat as she ran off after the thief.

Mr. Bellini, who was quite startled, wanted an apology.

Shouting, "STOP! STOP! STOP!" Mr.
Bellini ran after Porkchop, the dog, and Angus Macaw,
the thief, whom Mr. Bellini didn't know was a thief.

Like every Saturday,
Officer Dowdy had settled
the neighborhood rucus and
was taking his break in the park. Officer Dowdy
heard shouts. He saw a man chasing a dog, who
was chasing a bird, doggedly. The dutiful Officer
Dowdy got on his horse, Lily, and set off after them.

By the time Officer Dowdy got to them he found Angus Macaw, the thief, and Porkchop, the dog, collapsed at Mr. Bellini's feet. Angus Macaw knew he was caught, so he emptied the silverware from his knapsack. Service for two and a half was all that remained. It was then that he remembered he hadn't mended the hole!

Well, the Smalls had been collecting their very tarnished, unused silverware as they followed the chase. "Arrest that jailbird!" they demanded when they arrived at the scene. "This was the first time I was ever a thief. I needed money to buy a plane ticket home," confessed a shamefaced Angus Macaw as he was handcuffed to Lily. But a moment later he exclaimed, "What a birdbrain I am! Who needs a plane?!" Then Angus Macaw, the first-time thief, apologized to Mr. Bellini and thanked him for ending the chase.

Officer Dowdy informed the Smalls that
Mr. Bellini had single-handedly captured the thief.
Officer Dowdy took out a medal (he always had one or two on hand
for such occasions) and pinned it on the blushing Mr. Bellini.

Mr. Bellini, the hero, accepted a reward from the Smalls, too. It was a coupon for a free pizza pie with pepperoni. "Thank you," Mr. Bellini beamed as he waved goodbye to them all. "I love pizza!"

"Wait, Mr. Hero!" Mrs. Small called out, "We'll walk with you."
But then Mr. Small decided he did not want to make the
long walk home carrying all that heavy, tarnished
silverware. Mrs. Small agreed and said she did not
want to have to clean it anymore. Elvira and
Napoleon Small said they preferred
eating with their fingers.

So the Smalls gave all their silverware to Angus Macaw! Officer Dowdy, who was quite astonished, unhandcuffed Angus Macaw, who was very grateful.

Since there was no longer a thief, the Smalls decided
Mr. Bellini was no longer a hero. They asked him to
return their free coupon and Officer Dowdy asked
Mr. Bellini to return the medal, too.
Mr. Bellini obliged.

Mr. Bellini was happy that Angus Macaw was no longer a thief, but he was a little disappointed. He certainly would have enjoyed that pizza, and it isn't every day that one is given a medal!

When Mr. Bellini arrived home Caruso was
happy to see him. Mr. Bellini was so sorry for being
late that he declared, "There is such a thing as a leash,
you know. Next Saturday we go to the park *together!*"

Like every Saturday, Mr. Bellini looked in Caruso's empty dish and said, "Well, well, Caruso! You ate all that food?! Guess it's time for more." Just as he was about to fill the dish the doorbell rang. Outside there was a large, flat box with his name written on it.

Inside the box Mr. Bellini found a glorious pepperoni, cheese and olive pizza with this note:

> *To a warmhearted, bird-loving man, thanks for taking a stand between me and that Porkchop. Best wishes, Angus Macaw, The X-Thief.*
> *P.S. I bought this pie with silverware!*

Mr. Bellini finished giving Caruso his food, and even gave him a little of the pizza. "A friend like Angus and a pizza like this are worth twenty medals!" smiled Mr. Bellini, who was simply delighted.

So was Caruso.